Hushtown
A Peaceful Community

Written by Elizabeth Massie
Illustrated by Amy Wummer

STECK-VAUGHN
COMPANY

A Division of Harcourt Brace & Company

www.steck-vaughn.com

Contents

Chapter One

Welcome to Hushtown

Sometimes we're so busy we don't notice that something is, well, different. Maybe that's why the Jingleson family didn't notice it at first.

Moving is hard work. All the packing makes a person very sleepy. In fact, Erin Jingleson and her brother Brian were sleeping in the back seat of their parents' van during most of the long ride. They were just waking up when they saw the town's sign.

Their new house was beautiful, so much nicer and bigger than their old house, with such a huge yard. Erin and Brian were sure all their new friends would want to come and play there every day.

So the children didn't grumble a bit about helping to move the boxes and suitcases into their new house on Whisper Lane. It had light blue shutters and a pale yellow roof. There were lilac bushes in the front yard and a big, shady oak tree in the backyard. Yes, Erin and Brian were excited. Maybe that's why they didn't notice that Hushtown was very, very different.

The children helped their parents unpack. They squealed with delight when they found their toys. They helped their father stack empty boxes in the dusty basement and giggled when one of the boxes tumbled to the floor. As the unpacking continued, everyone laughed and called to each other to "look at this" and "did you see that?" No one thought anyone was being noisy.

But the neighbors seemed to think otherwise. The quiet folks of Hushtown peeked out windows and over hedges at the new neighbors.

Erin and Brian were so excited about the new house that they couldn't help but want to play, especially in the new yard. At least there weren't any boxes in it.

Brian said to his sister, "Let's go make some new friends!" Out the door and down the street they went.

There were many children playing in their yards on Whisper Lane. Brian and Erin waved to a girl who was sitting on her porch with her doll.

"Hello!" called Erin. "I'm Erin Jingleson and this is my brother Brian. Would you like to play kickball?"

"Oh," said the girl in a very quiet voice. "That would make too much noise."

Erin and Brian just stared at each other.

At a second house, two boys were playing checkers.

"Would you like to jump rope?" Brian asked.

"We can't play that kind of game," said one boy softly as he looked down at the ground.

At a third house, a girl was holding out a treat for her little spotted terrier. While the dog sat up on its legs, it looked like it barked, but no sound came out.

"Good morning!" said Erin. "Do you want to play tag?"

"Tag?" whispered the girl. "What's tag?"

"Haven't you ever played tag?" asked Brian. "It's the best! You run and yell and try to catch each other."

"Tag sounds much too noisy," said the girl. "I'm sorry, but I can't play." She quickly went in the house. The door didn't even bang. Everything was so quiet, it was strange. Erin looked at Brian.

"This is weird!" Brian said as they walked home.

7

Erin and Brian went back home and sat in their backyard. They were confused. Everyone seemed friendly, but no one wanted to play with them. Erin and Brian started to notice that something was a little funny in Hushtown. Nothing seemed to make sense.

"Well, at least we've got each other," said Brian. "I guess we'll have to think of something we can do."

"I have an idea," said Erin. "The oak tree in the backyard is really big, and the branches are just right, so why don't we build a tree house? Maybe then the children we saw will want to play with us."

Brian said, "Yeah. I bet if we build a really neat tree house, all the kids will want to see it."

Chapter Two

Erin and Brian's Plan

Under the cobwebs in the basement, Erin and Brian found a box of nails, two hammers, and some warped boards.

They went to work right away. They worked all day, putting boards here and there.

Whack! Bam! Smack! Slam!

When they were finished, they wiggled around in the tree house. It was quite uncomfortable.

"I wish our tree house was better. No one is going to come over to play in this," said Erin.

"Hello," came a soft voice. Erin and Brian turned to see someone standing there.

"I heard you making noise. What in the world are you doing in that tree?" asked the lady.

"We're building a tree house," said Erin with a sigh. "We want it to be great."

"I see. Well, my name is Mrs. Mutter. I'm your next door neighbor," said the lady. Then she looked around as if she didn't want anyone else to hear her and said, "I could help you if you'd like. I'm a science teacher. Maybe I could help you design a better tree house."

"Would you really help us?" asked Brian.

"Please," said Erin. "No one likes our games or anything. Do you know what the kids here like to do to have fun?"

Mrs. Mutter looked at Erin sadly. She whispered, "This is Hushtown. Everything in Hushtown is supposed to be quiet."

Then Mrs. Mutter went into her house and returned with graph paper and markers. Together, they drew a plan for the best tree house ever.

The markers squeaked, and the paper rattled. Mrs. Mutter chuckled until she laughed. "I've always wanted to see a tree house in Hushtown,"

she said. "But everything here is supposed to be quiet. I guess people thought a tree house would be too noisy. Planning this tree house is the most fun I've had in a long time!"

Erin looked Mrs. Mutter right in the eyes. "Mrs. Mutter, why is everyone so quiet? It's like they're afraid to make any sounds at all!"

Mrs. Mutter stopped in surprise. Then she sighed and began the story.

"Actually, it's a very old story—so old no one really remembers all of it."

Brian said, "Please tell us."

So Mrs. Mutter told them how the hush came to Hushtown.

Mrs. Mutter began, "Old Mr. Jangle used to own the biggest factory in town. The factory made noisemakers, such as bells, whistles, horns, and sirens. You name it, Mr. Jangle's factory made a noisy dinger or whizzer for it. It made toys, cars, alarms for stores, and even oven buzzers for bakers. People worked in the factory around the clock.

"Such racket came from the factory! No one could sleep, the children couldn't study, and the birds couldn't hear themselves sing. One family after another left our town, and it was very sad indeed.

"Then old Mr. Muffle, our Mayor Muffle's grandfather, went from his little shop one day to see Mr. Jangle. Mr. Muffle's shop made earmuffs, earplugs, and headphones. When it was cold, Mr. Muffle's earmuffs kept people's ears warm, and when they had to do noisy jobs, they ordered Mr. Muffle's earplugs.

"Next we knew, Mr. Jangle moved away. No one ever knew exactly why or what happened. But we knew that Mr. Muffle bought the noisy factory. Soon Mr. Muffle had the workers making earmuffs, earplugs, and headphones.

"Pretty soon, folks made new laws about sounds and even renamed the town Hushtown. Then people started to move back into town, so everyone seemed happy. But sometimes I think Hushtown is too quiet."

Mrs. Mutter stood up and said, "It's late. We'll have to work more on the tree house tomorrow."

13

The next morning, Brian and Erin asked their father to take them to Mr. Mumble's Lumber Yard.

Mr. Mumble smiled at the plans. "A tree house?" he whispered. "I've always wanted to see a tree house in Hushtown. I guess no one ever built one because they thought it would be too noisy. Let me get you some wood."

Board after board went into the van.

Plank! Plunk! Plop!

Mr. Jingleson drove carefully with the load of wood. The boards rattled, shook, and banged together. Other drivers stared and frowned. Children on the sidewalks covered their ears.

The wood squeaked when they turned corners. The van's brakes groaned when they stopped for a light. The back door thumped on the wood when they went over the tiniest bumps in the road.

Brian sang, and Erin whistled. To them, this wasn't noise but just the sounds of everyday life.

Chapter Three

What's the Noise About?

Back at the tree, Erin and Brian followed the plan they had made with Mrs. Mutter. They nailed a plank here and nailed a plank there.

Whack! Smack! Bam! Slam!

An alarmed police officer rushed into the yard. She called to the children, "What is going on?" But she was talking too softly for Erin and Brian to hear.

The officer went back to her car to get the bullhorn. She had never used it before because it was way, way too loud.

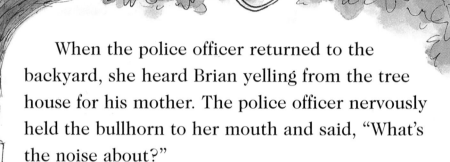

When the police officer returned to the backyard, she heard Brian yelling from the tree house for his mother. The police officer nervously held the bullhorn to her mouth and said, "What's the noise about?"

Brian stopped yelling and looked at the officer. He said, "We're building a tree house, officer."

The officer replied, "Well, you need to keep it down. This is Hushtown, you know."

"Yes, officer," said Brain. "I was calling my mom."

"In that case, you might as well keep this bullhorn. But use it when you have to," she said.

Brian and Erin thanked the police officer and mounted the bullhorn to a branch. Then they pushed the button and tried it out.

"Howdy," said a fire fighter, who came running into the yard. "I just got a call about the noise in your backyard. Oh, now I see what all the noise is about. You're building a tree house. You know, you should use a sturdy ladder to get up and down that tree. It's much safer than crawling up those steps." With that, the fire fighter took his ladder from his truck and set it against the tree.

"Let me show you how to climb it," he told Brian and Erin. The fire fighter demonstrated how to safely go up and down the ladder. Then he had Erin and Brian practice.

"This is super!" said Erin.

"Thank you very much!" said Brian.

17

The next morning Erin and Brian were working in the tree house when a boy and his father came to the Jingleson's yard. The father was carrying a large box.

"Hi," said the boy shyly. "My name is Vince, and this is my father. We live across the street, and we've been watching you build the tree house. Can we help?"

"Of course!" said Erin and Brian together.

Vince's father opened the box. Inside there was a pulley, a strong rope, and a swing seat.

Brian asked, "What's that for?"

Vince replied, "You'll see. My dad's a mechanic, and he can make anything. He has an idea that will make your tree house really cool."

"I can't wait to see what it is!" said Brian.

With a bit of hammering and bolting, Vince's father went to work. Before long he had built an elevator. Erin, Brian, and Vince watched as Vince's father made the elevator go up and down to the tree house with a tug of the rope.

"Wow! You did it. The elevator is great. Now our tree house will be the best!" shouted Erin and Brian. Even Vince and Vince's father cheered, to the surprise of the neighbors.

19

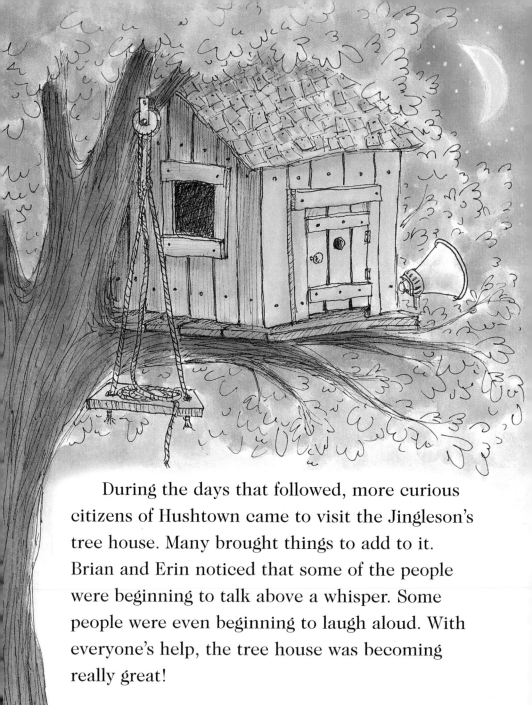

During the days that followed, more curious citizens of Hushtown came to visit the Jingleson's tree house. Many brought things to add to it. Brian and Erin noticed that some of the people were beginning to talk above a whisper. Some people were even beginning to laugh aloud. With everyone's help, the tree house was becoming really great!

Chapter Four

Furniture, Lights, and Mail, Oh My!

One morning, Mr. Mummer parked his truck at the Jingleson's house. He walked into the backyard to see a huge tree house.

Mr. Mummer called up to the children, "I like your tree house. But where's its furniture?"

"We can't build furniture," said Erin.

"Well, I can. I'm the best carpenter in town," said Mr. Mummer.

Then he walked back to his truck. A little later, he returned with his tools and a load of wood.

Mr. Mummer worked with his hammer and saw. When he was done, he had built a wonderful table and two chairs for the tree house.

At noon, Mrs. Jingleson went out to get the mail. The mail carrier was at the mailbox and asked, "Have you heard that there's a tree house around here?"

Mrs. Jingleson giggled and said, "I sure have. My children are building it." She led the mail carrier back to the tree house and introduced her to Erin and Brian.

The mail carrier smiled and said, "Hello, there. What a wonderful place! I bet you'll be wanting to get your mail up there."

"I hope someone will write us," said Erin.

Then the mail carrier went out to her truck and returned with a shiny bucket with a small red flag.

"Hang this on your branch," she said. "When there is mail, I will turn up your flag, and you'll know." She flipped up the flag, and it began to *twirl.*

22

Day after day, all the children in Hushtown were talking about the tree house. More and more neighbors came over to see it. Even children from way across town dropped by just to take a look.

The tree house just kept getting better. One day the electrician from Hush Up Lights 'N Stuff pulled up in his truck and hauled a box of tools to the backyard.

"Everybody is talking about your tree house," he said. "And I think it's great! I have something to give it a finishing touch."

He began to place wires all around the tree.

Bang! Bang! Bang!

The electrician pounded the nails around the outside of the tree house. Then he strung up one long wire from nail to nail. The wire wrapped around the tree house.

"Now," said the electrician, putting his finger to a switch he'd mounted to the side of the tree, "Watch what happens!"

Lights of every imaginable color lit up around the tree house.

Just then all the neighbors came into the yard and looked at the most wonderful, most glorious tree house in the whole world.

"Ah!" everyone said together. "Wow!" everyone said as they clapped their hands. "Look at what we've done by working together."

Chapter Five

Mayor Muffle Pays a Visit

A very grumpy, very grouchy, yet very quiet voice came from the back of the crowd. It asked, "What is all this disturbance?"

Everyone turned to see a tall woman with a sharp nose. Her eyes were narrow. Her hands were tight on her hips.

Everyone stopped clapping and stood there in silence.

"Mayor Muffle," whispered one of the neighbors.

"Oh, dear!" someone else said softly.

"I've come to see the tree house," said Mayor Muffle, her voice muffled through tightly pressed lips. "I heard all this racket. I want to know what is going on. I've come to investigate the noise."

Mayor Muffle turned around and eyed the tree house. "Now, let me take a closer look."

Nobody moved as Mayor Muffle walked around the base of the tree. Everyone held their breath as she stood on tip-toe to look inside. Nobody spoke as she rubbed her chin and shook her head and crossed her arms and tapped her foot. Then she reached into her pocket and pulled out her magnifying glass. She carefully studied the tree house from top to bottom. She did not look happy. Everyone waited to see what would happen.

Then Mayor Muffle turned around and faced the crowd. Her face began to soften. Her mouth began to tremble. Her narrow eyes began to widen. She placed her magnifying glass back inside her pocket.

"Goodness gracious," she said in her still-quiet voice. "This is a wonderful tree house. It has lights, furniture, a mailbox, a ladder, a bullhorn, windows, a door, and so much more. It's the first tree house I've ever seen in Hushtown. And best of all, everyone in town helped to build it!"

She began to smile, and then she began to laugh. The whole town celebrated.

Chapter Six

Read All About It!

The following morning the Hushtown Times ran an editorial on the front page. It was written by the mayor. Brian, Erin, and the neighborhood children sat in the tree house reading the editorial.

Hushtown Times

Today's News

Due to the construction of a very fine tree house on Whisper Lane, I have decided that some sound within the city limits of Hushtown is acceptable. The sound of people working together is nice. I like that kind of sound in Hushtown. Thank you, Erin and Brian Jingleson and citizens of Hushtown!

Yours truly,
Mayor Margaret Muffle

Brian looked out of the tree house and said, "Hey, the red flag is up! We have mail."

Vince lowered Brian in the elevator, and he pulled out the envelope. It looked official, with a seal from the mayor's office on the return address.

"It's from Mayor Muffle," said Brian as he opened the envelope.

City of Hushtown

Official Mail

Dear Brian and Erin Jingleson,

The town council met last night. All we could talk about was the way everyone worked together to build your fine tree house. Then we wondered about other ideas that could bring our townspeople together. That is when we decided that our town needs some music. But first we need a bandstand. Would you be in charge of our first official community project?

Sincerely,

Mayor Muffle

Brian, Erin, and Mrs. Mutter used graph paper and markers to draw a plan for Hushtown's new bandstand. Mr. Mumble, Vince's dad, Mr. Mummer, Erin and Brian's parents, the police officer, the fire fighter, the electrician, and all the citizens of Hushtown helped to build it. Everyone, even the children, worked together. When the work was finished, Hushtown had a fantastic bandstand for its park!

The first community concert had lots of squeaks and even more squawks. At first, Mayor Muffle wore earmuffs. But the band got better. Before long, Hushtown invited the people of Riverview, a nearby town, to their concert.

After the first concert, Mayor Muffle asked Brian and Erin to come with her to the edge of town. There they repainted the town's sign.

Welcome to
Hushtown
A Peaceful
Community
Full of
Happy Sounds